For My Grand-daughter

Macey Jay

With Love

MOTHER OF KINGS

Mother of Kings

When happiness enters one's life, the years fly by so quickly leaving many memories of sadness to fade into the dark nights of sleep. I will always remember my hidden secret of long past and the sadness I endured. They belong to my memory, dreams and nightmares. For you alone I will share my secret which is a puzzle in my mind of imagination. Read my written words carefully and take yourself beyond the boundaries of life. Will you be able to see what I see or know what I know? Can you find that missing piece of puzzle that will put the stories of torment to rest? So make of my story what you will. Let my written words enter your imagination and maybe your soul will run wild with a hunger to know. Make sense of the senseless and ask yourself, where would you want me to be. For my soul is asking you to be my guardian.

I am not prepared to mention names or dates as my recollection of past events must still in some way be concealed. My name I will not share with you! I want you to think I could be anyone, even yourself. I assure you! You will be able to guess my name and question events. Try not to forget anything is possible in life as in death. So empty your mind of thoughts. Read on!

Garden of Dreams

Looking out from my bedroom window down into the garden below, I again could see that heavenly hue. A mist of angels wings falling to cover and protect the gentle flowers of all colours, which are scattered across the garden of dreams. Each flower stretched their head trying to reach the sun above, so pretty it was as though a rainbow hoop had fallen from the sky and painted their petals.

A fountain of life will sprinkle water so the drops can quench the gardens thirst. On the right bordering my garden is an army of trees in regimental order. They stand at ease in their green leaf armour, swaying gently with the passing breeze. Their branches become the shadowy weapons which lay across the sloping lawn below, protecting my home from the sea storms. So tall the trees, but towering above them merging into the reckless sky is the sea. She is deep and unpredictable her depth holds the beauty and innocence of a newborn child. Her waves of emotion lap around my island of rocks and sandy beaches, which are protected and cherished by the distant coral reefs. They fill life with many wonders which makes one realize the power of Mother Nature's Creation.

Straight ahead are the green sweeping hills, some tipped with a soft white snow. They seem to dip to form a valley. Through the heart of the valley bedded deep is a river reflecting memories gone by and flowing with future dreams towards the untamed sea. When clouds of lace pass over and burst they shower the earth with raindrops, the river runs fast to collect every drop of water that falls. I sometimes imagine the river is the collector of human tears.

Is my island heaven or earth? I only know my home is a home of happiness and safety. No one can find me or touch me. I live here to love and be loved. It is what my soul; has always craved for.

Far away in the distant sky a storm is brewing, threatening to block out the shining sun. Clouds push themselves together forming a look alike mountainous range reaching high into the sky. Thunder rumbles so loud it echoes through the valley. The whole sky lights up as the lightning flashes. Reminding me of those flashing cameras that once invaded my private life. The media would do anything to photograph me, there was no stopping them. They acted like creatures from out of space, fighting for a specimen of human tragedy.

The storm in the distant sky turns away from my island but those flashes of lightening reminded me that today many years ago I died to live. A decision made for me to smile for life and to love again, keeping my dignity.

Night time was drawing in and the scent of flowers filled the air, which reminded me of my last farewell. I was filled with sadness as the past loneliness returned to haunt me. That haunting brought back the city of life but it came with an unearthly silence in the air (lifeless) there was no movement, even the morning songbirds were silent and hidden from view. It was as though an angel had passed over the city taking away all earthly sounds, leaving an empty echo. There was no movement. It seemed to be a dead city. This day was the day of my funeral and maybe the city had died with me or was it mourning my last farewell. I seemed to wander around looking for life. Then from that empty echo I could hear a shouting of orders and marching as though a thousand feet hit the ground stamping together in perfect rhythm, gently shaking the city as though they were trying to wake it. A regiment of men began to line a route which was to take me on my final journey on this earth. Still there was that unearthly silence even when people began to fill empty spaces behind the lines of guards. I walked through the crowds unnoticed, no one gave me a second glance, why would they? But I am sure I can recall a small child giving me a yellow rose and then running away. Maybe it was a spirit child but I assure you it did make me feel more alive, just to know someone had seen me.

Grief and sadness was on everyone's face. Was it because I was so young or loved by so many? Tears were rolling down everyone's cheeks. Before they fell to the ground they all seemed to turn blue with the reflection of the sky. As each tear fell I could hear a ring as though death had turned them to ice, or was it the bells of heaven calling for me? I must have touched everyone's heart including the angels. There were so many flowers, flowers for me. There could not have been a flower in any shop left in the kingdom. Every flower had a sad face but still produced that heavenly perfume and colours of life creating a carpet of beauty so vast. I was honoured with the simplest of life nature can hold. I held tight the rose the little child gave me, you see I needed to know I was alive.

An uncanny scent filled the air, which made my emotion over take logic, I saw the flowers I had on my wedding day. A day I remember well.

A cold chill went down my spine as everyone stood still and silent. There was a far distant echo of horses' hooves pounding the roads with their metal shoes as if in a slow march. A single drum was beating pacing the hooves of steel. It seemed to get nearer and nearer and then I could hear again the marching of a thousand feet. I had to get nearer to see, I pushed through the crowds nobody moved out of my way, it was as though I was a ghost walking through everyone. Then I saw those beautiful proud black horses, their heads held high with a black plume which shimmered as the breeze passed through. The shine on their coats made every muscle in their body ripple as it pulled the heavy carriage holding my coffin. As they passed their heads turned towards me, they snorted as if to acknowledge my form.

It was a funeral fit for a queen or a Mother of Kings. Then I saw my children walking behind the coffin. How young they looked with a proud determination of calmness on their faces. Their father walked by their side, he was now their full protector. I wanted to shout to touch them. Tears came to my eyes and I began to panic. Did I remember to tell them, am I really here or did the plan go wrong? I tried to get over the barrier and past the guards to reach them. Then everything went black. Maybe I passed out, I don't know. Then I felt as though I was surrounded by murky water, alone on an island. An island of nothing filled only with thoughts that had made my soul a prisoner. I cried out for help, I heard my father call me. But how could that be. Then out of nothing came a hand and arm beckoning me. Taking hold of the hand the darkness turned to light. Maybe I fell into a deep sleep of dreams a light brought a vivid memory of my wedding day which then came to view.

Fate's Plan

The world was waiting for my wedding day! I was that fairytale princess every girl dreamed of being. My wedding dress was priceless and designed in the most exquisite fashion. I lifted my wedding dress to reveal my silken shoes, as I stepped into the golden carriage which was pulled by white horses. They trotted in joy and followed the ringing bells towards the steps of the cathedral. As I walked down the aisle, my silk gown rustled as though the silk worms were still producing that needed silk of purest white. The bodice glistened with sparkling jewels, which fitted perfectly. Even a spider would have been jealous of my lace veil. It hung from my head sparkling with the early morning dewdrops. My diamond tiara glowing with all the colours of a rainbow, held my veil securely as the length draped the aisle. I was crowned with glory. I held my flowers of nature's own perfection so tight with nerves and excitement. Each step took me towards a new future. As I moved closer to the alter, I tried to imagine all the love I had ahead of me. Not for one moment did I realize that fate had another plan for me. Maybe I became the light of youth in an old fashioned family. This was not their fault but the unchanging system of protocol.

You only saw a fashion icon, beautiful and a coy smile that could hypnotize any newspaper editor. Did anyone know what was going on in my mind? I doubt it. The spirit of my soul became a prisoner waiting to be tamed (like a wild animal) to fit into a society, which many would envy. To break a spirit one can just about cope but when your heart breaks as well every emotion shatters. I became lost looking into the world of sadness. I wanted to tread a road of danger so a child could follow my footsteps in safety and to touch a child no one could cuddle and love. To shake a hand of the unshakeable. This I did and do you know my spirit began to repair with each smile from those little earth angels. I was their hope and they my healer. I knew fate had directed me.

I suppose subconsciously I knew it would be a difficult marriage as my husband was much older than myself and we did not share common interests. After our second child our marriage began to fail rapidly.

Whose fault was it, only ourselves can say. But I always thought my husband was in love with another of long standing. My thoughts of revenge overtook my logical mind. I was out to destroy. They say woe is a woman scorned! I thought that was me! I pulled my husband to pieces with insinuations and comments, which gave the media a field day. Any uncertain future can confuse one's mind and way of thinking. It is a fear of being alone, which creates a void and every moment a hidden anger makes you want to fight to keep a broken relationship. Or destroy a partner before the final parting divorce. I now realized after all these years our marriage together was the most complemented any woman could have. You see, I was chosen to be the mother of his children. So love shows itself in many different ways. I also know if I had succeeded in destroying him. I would have destroyed my children's future as well. That would be unforgivable.

One wonders if I was afraid to find true happiness, not really knowing what to look for but I did. They say love conquers worlds. Well at last I conquered my world. I found that magic moment of true love and an unconditional relationship, for once in my life I no longer have that empty feeling. There were rumours that protocol would deny me the right to remarry. Maybe they would have preferred me to enter a convent, just out of sight and sound!

This gave me the strength to disappear and let go of my identity. A plan to change my life into a life of freedom. There was no way I was going to be caged to be tamed. It was now my time! Secret agents were called in to arrange the details.

Before I go any further, I want you all to know, I gave you all fair warning! After all what would anyone think if they heard someone say, to live my life, I would have to live in a remote country where no one can recognize me. The second more profound statement was, in a few months news will be announced that will shock the world. I think everyone thought I was going to marry or even announce I was pregnant. Now remember what shock means, sudden and violent! It was obvious I knew what was going to happen. So like I say you all had fair warning. New identities were put into place with great care and secrecy. There could be no flaw in my future. I found it very difficult at first to memorize all what I was being told but it soon fell into place. Now was the time for my new future to begin. Hidden well for six months in a scrap yard was the car, which became part of the plan. This was to take me on my final destination. That long awaited dream became a nightmare. A storm raged outside with an unearthly anger. The wind blew as though heaven had opened her door with fury, everything in her wake was bruised from the unforeseen force. The rain fell horizontally cutting everything in its path with an iced chill. It was as though heaven was fighting for my soul or showing me the emotions of life.

It was the early hours of the morning, when I left the hotel with my love by my side. We were on our way to our new home. There would be little or no traffic on the road. From that moment, time seemed to have stopped. That turning door seemed to be a time machine just waiting to take me through the galaxy. No longer was a storm raging threatening my existence. I had entered a silent zone. I was travelling in a car that had jumped over those storm clouds, into the galaxy of stars. Shimmering dust from the stars became a pathway for me to follow, they twinkled with excitement as I passed them by. I thought I was on my way to heaven as I danced with the stars. I wanted to take one and put it in my pocket. Then I began to fall from the universal splendour. The silent zone was no longer silent. I heard the rushing of waves from the sea. I sank into the magic of blue dreams. The rushing of waves racing towards the sandy shore seemed to beckon me to look towards the blue horizon. I was hypnotized by the sun sparkling in each ripple. Then it came into view, a yacht bobbing up and down with the swell of the sea tides. It seemed to invite me to board her. I just couldn't wait to stand on her deck. I then knew there was no turning back. The yacht raced towards the horizon until it reached its destination. My island of happiness.

It is so peaceful here, no longer do I need the materialistic things of life and I have become in harmony with nature. Sometimes I wonder, is it just my spirit that touches the earth, who knows! I only know reality, real life can sometimes be cruel.

I still have nightmares when I sleep but not so regular. I suppose that is part of living no one wants. It's like being haunted by oneself.

A newspaper, television program and even what I am writing triggers off the hurt in life and unrests my soul, knowing also I have left many unanswered questions and a plan that was imperfect, 'or was it?'.

It's strange as the nightmare very rarely changes. It seems as though it is never ending. I see myself going through a turning door only to go into a hall with a large mirror I cannot distinguish who is the real me. I even try to touch the mirror, but my hands feel no cold glass only an ice cold hand. Pulling my hand away quickly I turn to see two doors, knowing only the real me can choose to open and walk through one. There are people watching, they see this magical illusion. I was terrified to open and choose a door but I had to, so I could get out of my dream. I chose the wrong door as an ice cold chill shivered down my spine as I entered it became dark, cold, damp and lonely. Not even my vision of the mirror was with me. I could feel wet sodden soil as though I had no shoes on. I wanted to scream but I couldn't even my tears froze with fear. There was my childhood home I could see it in the distance but I could not escape to reach it. Panicking I ran to and fro, round and round only to find I was surrounded by water. Was I on that island of nothing. How could my sleep time be so cruel. I wanted to wake but my nightmare relentlessly carried on. Dawn began to break and there they were the spiders. They were weaving their webs for the morning dew and next meal. They were weaving around my feet crawling upwards the sticky webs covering my skin. They were going to devour me! I started thrashing out with my hands trying to brush them away but still they kept coming and still weaving. I fell to the ground but knew I had to drag myself to the water's edge to wash them away. There was a bedraggled rat on the edge it jumped into a whirlpool and I followed then within a split second I was in my home. Then a piercing screech came from behind me, I turned, and scurrying was the rat it was bedraggled and dirty. It became a scavenger searching through my belongings and then began to consume them. He started to grow which turned him into a monster of greed. There was nothing left, he turned to look at me. His fanged teeth were yellow with age, he was frothing at the mouth. Evil was those red eyes, they belonged to someone I most trusted. I called that name it screeched and sprang towards my throat, he was that fat he hit my chest with a thud. Always at that moment I wake. Some days I look into this nightmare and it could have been a warning for my life.

Pendulum of Time

I cannot seem to get rid of that knocking in my head. It is as though something is frantically trying to get out or escape from a confused mind. I feel as though I am going mad, knock! knock! It seems to echo with time I begin to wonder 'who am I, where am I?' I try to open my eyes they seem reluctant to move, as though they were frozen with time, I rubbed them hard with my hands, they slowly opened only to see a face of fear knocking with his hands on the window of a car in which I was sitting. He was shouting in a foreign language 'open the door! open the door!' How on earth did I get into the car? Has my memory gone or was I once again having those futuristic visions.

Chaos is outside of the car people begin to look in. The car door opens and someone pulls me out. I look around only to see that magical illusion of myself, sitting in the back of the car. Was I having an out of body experience?

I turned around to look at the illusion of myself but it never moved, I was holding my arm as I was in so much pain, so it could not have been me.

The hair colour, clothes, the shoes, THE SHOES! They are not mine, that is not me but who would willingly take my place? I was taken away to another vehicle it seemed like the one that took me into the galaxy of stars, from that moment on I never turned back, but still I don't know if that was the day I died.

Death! The word no one wants to know about or do we subconsciously. Maybe the sleeping spirit begins to awake to work and learn about the unimaginable universal clock. The dreams, visions and nightmares do they become the clocks pendulum swinging back and forth with the essence of time. Until the eyelids open, waking the unconscious mind from the deep sleep of nothing. Each second that ticks away is a manmade movement making dreams visual. We are all born to live and die but will our spirit return and rewind past memories.

Was death another vision of my future? Is it still possible I am alive? I sometimes think I have died before in time gone by but no one wanted to put me at rest away from the ticking of the manmade clock.

I still also vividly see the funeral fit for a queen or

Mother of Kings. So was I really in that coffin? Maybe someone out there can remember seeing me on that day.

The sun begins to set bringing the dusk, and the shadows of night begin to appear. Where do they come from? It is as though every flower, tree and garden creature plays hide and seek on my lawn. The dark night sky sends out beams of light and my garden pool has captured all the stars. I look to see that man in the moon smiling at me I just stare and dream everything is dancing. Oh! I loved my dancing! I miss it so much. That comment is scary, why would I have stopped dancing. It is something that has not crossed my mind until now.

I know I listen to music, strange music. Some would say it could be language of the angels or the music of Gods. There is a haunting melody which touches my heart the most. It is ghostly and when I hear it, it seems as though it passes through my body. Perhaps that is me dancing. I do feel as though I have heard this music before. It comes as soon as I close my shutters and switch on the lights. Always the lights flicker like the flames of a candle dancing. I lay my head on the satin pillow to sleep.

Always I wake to watch the early morning sea mist, rolling in like a giant wave as though it is ready to consume all in its path. Within seconds nature has hidden the beauty of the sea covering her with a blanket of danger. Everything becomes still and eerie as the wave of mist reaches my island, bringing with it a cold damp feeling. For just one moment of time, I can no longer see my garden of dreams. I am scared, scared of seeing nothing. I begin to feel as though I have been taken away and hidden so no one could find me. Have I gone mad? My mind begins to play games as the white swirling sea mist begins to distort as a gentle breeze passes through. Shapes begin to appear with a supernatural force. I sit watching wanting to make these shapes into stories to evade my fear of nothing. I allow my pure imagination to work to give the answers I am looking for. It seems as though my imagination is more profound than I realized. The shapes seem to represent past, present and future events. How would it be possible to see the future, maybe heaven is my home!

I begin to scry the mist with thoughts of my children. The mist twists into a vision of two warriors, proudly they walk together. Each differs in looks and status, their clothes and headdress are of different tribes. Whirling above them are the blades of glory. They separate and walk into two different paths. One path leads to the sea the other a desert. Following behind are an army of young warriors they each hold a flag of many nations. Are my children going to war? I don't know. I reach out to touch them but the sea mist moves quickly and the vision changes into many children. Each child carries a tree filled with fruit. The trees have been grown to replant forests around the world. They are trees of life.

Again the mist turns to reveal a female of much beauty. Her eyes are as bright as the stars, she wears a crown but it is not the crown of a queen. At her feet are three children two boys and one girl. The girl wears a crown of many jewels, she will be queen her strength is great and men will fall at her feet for her beauty and wisdom. As the sea mist begins to clear it leaves drops of water on the faces of the family. They become the tears of angels who cry for humanity. Before the sea mist disappears the younger warrior appears holding a dove in his hands, he lets it fly towards my island. All disappears and nature throws off her blanket to reveal again my island of dreams and the deep blue sea. I begin to wonder where the elder of the warrior king has gone. Maybe he will come again in one of my visions or my imagination. My mind begins, again, to work overtime.

There are many questions to be answered, as many people think I died in a sinister way (if I did die)! Even I myself need answers. I would like to know who would hate me so much to want to see me dead! One could look to the obvious but I know they would not hurt my children so much, for their love for them is great. Also there is one out there who needs answers more than myself. His wealth cannot mend his broken heart as a branch from his tree of life has been cut down. Even many exotic gifts cannot ease his pain, he also grieves for me. Sometimes when I scry the sea mist, I see this man sitting with his head in his hands, rocking back and forth with sorrow. Sitting by his side is a tiger who was captured from a jungle in the north east of Asia. He lifts his head to look into the tigers magical eyes, as she sees all. So wild she begins to race across land and sea it's as though she is a shooting star as she leaves the universe her claws reach out to take a horn of plenty from the star dust. She comes to the seas of many tides and mighty waves. Then drops the horn which falls onto my island. I am uneasy to know she has found my sanctuary. Would the one who grieves so much be safe if he knew the real secret?

Just for one second I turn away only to look back at the mighty sea of seas turning into a water spout which began to form, a shape of a serpent. A lashing tail began to froth the stormy seas. Its body was long with blue and green scales. It has two heads they cannot keep still. One head tries to hide behind the other but one could see it was a woman of age. Around her neck is a necklace of pearls from the bed of an oyster. Her hair was that of sea snakes. They wriggled to tidy themselves. Hollow sockets were her eyes but you could see and smell jealously. It was as though someone had taken something that was to be hers. Was she the one capable of destroying me? If so she has taken her secret to the grave. She turns her head with rage trying to protect her identity, lashing out at the other head. This head is male to see his face is alarming as one cannot mistake his identity. He is one who gave away power only to take it to a higher level. He has hands which he holds together as if in prayer, praying for forgiveness but it is to hide his synion line. Even through sadness and times of disaster he keeps the smile upon his face with eyes that stare as though he has no emotion. This man has a greedy evil; plan as he pushes you all into submission. As whilst you sleep he would be capable of devouring your children, just to keep his own safe. I will tell you this man's greed will not go unnoticed if he really exists.

Deep in the water of the lake in the grounds of my childhood home from a distance you would think a piece of glass had fallen from heaven and laid itself upon the ground, for the angels to dance upon. As they danced, from their wings, they dropped the seeds of nature to dress the lake, for all seasons. In the middle is an island, If I look towards it, a cold chill goes down my spine and often I can see a ghostly figure, moving back and forth in the moonlight. It seems to beckon me and I turn away quickly.

Branches hang over the lake from the tree that weeps. It is a majestic giant of all trees and its pale green leaves seem to want to watch their reflection in the lakes deep still water. The trunk of the tree has a face of a wise old man. He is one who has collected many secrets for centuries, keeping them safe for the souls of man.

I would stand by him and believe he had opened his eyes and was talking to me. Always saying 'My child you hold many secrets and you are your ancestors dream, a Mother of Kings but not a queen nor the lady of the lake. You will hide a great secret and your face from mankind. So sad! So sad! You will be like a flower, picked and tossed aside before your beauty is in full bloom. He looked down at me and smiled and said the strangest thing, that when the great mountain of the north erupts with anger, people will sleep. When they wake we will be forgotten. I shared much with the wise old man he was a fantasy seer. He still stands proud and tall by the side of the lake.

Mask of Sorrow

Story after story and still no one has dug deep enough to find the real truth. Are they afraid of the worms that turn, who will leave a slither of poison behind them.

Buried deep beneath the unhallowed ground on the island of the lake is a heavy metal coffin. It has the crest with a unicorns head above and is sealed to hide the contents. What is within? It is not me! That I am sure.

Time and many years will pass by and my children's children will be born to watch the waters of the kingdom rise, then so will the coffin. It will become a Pandora's box, waiting to be opened, releasing much of nothing. Only thoughts and imagination will wait to escape, it was a coffin of deceit!

Maybe there is another story you should hear about. It is purely fictitious, but it does no harm to pretend, unless of course there is an element of truth. There is a home that once belonged to the unforgiven. A man who lost all for the sake of love. His heart was filled with sorrow when he left his country (never to return). Banished from a kingdom that was once his, he found sanctuary in the remote home in the hills of France. He married his love as she was his life, living together (childless) until it was their time to pass to another world. The home became empty and seemed lost in time. It held the ghosts of the past within its walls, with a promise to release them when a love of life would take their place.

How could that not be the perfect home for me as I wanted life and had so much love to give. Thus this home became a gift of devotion and the home became mine letting the ghost of the past, free to travel on together to eternity.

That fatal night we were on our way to move into our new home. The journey was long and tiring, so we stopped off at the hotel to rest, just to break the journey.

It was a strange night as forces of the unforeseen was all around. At first I thought it was a warning not to share my home with the ghosts of the past. I even wondered if the house wanted to stay empty, to haunt.

Then came the pain I hurt so much, it was as though I was in childbirth. Next I am in a car that is racing, taking me to the hospital. I'm wanting the car to slow down as through the pain I could not put my safety belt on. Next I am in a hospital. A hospital which I was to be booked in, later on in the month.

Come now! Think! What would you want for me? An unconventional joy for me would have to be disguised by a mask of sorrow. The mask of the grim reaper was chosen to hide my joy. Was the grim reaper behind the mask? From that moment on my life became a fairytale with no end.

Not for one moment did anyone think how people would react to the news of sorrow. It was devastation which left everyone in turmoil. Not looking for a happier ending left an error of judgment, to those who could have prevented the mask of the grim reaper to be worn. Everyone thrived on the sorrow not one look further for joy. That was a big mistake. Perhaps someone out there should search for written certificates of proof, for the joy of life to give a happy ending to a fairytale.

War of the Heavens

I hear the clock ticking it never stops, the pendulum swings back and forth marking the seconds, minutes and hours. They move forward to the days, months and years. A giant step of time has passed, everything has changed, people age. But I seem to stand still like the outer case of the clock.

I never age or grow old even though the seasons of nature have passed me by, many times.

The clouds overhead would gently surf the summer blue sky, making me want to fly with time. There then becomes a race against the elements as the clouds become curtains, draping the blue sky. They display their shapes in full force, thanking summer for her hospitality, is as though they are alive! They know autumn's magic is nearby.

This always makes me feel uneasy as no matter how many people are around the autumn chill brings loneliness with that comes the dark nights and the predators. Through my vulnerability to kindness, they wounded and froze my heart. I fell to the earth like a fallen sparrow into a bush of brambles. Not even being able to move, from fear and the thorns. Above me were the magpies looking for something shiny to feed their ego. They swooped and squawked for all to see and hear, trying to become rich from my tragic events. I begin to panic and see the ghosts of the earth gathering around the brambles they are looking for me, not knowing I am the fallen sparrow. They cannot find me beneath the unhallowed ground. I somehow sense the living and the dead will not rest until I am found. The dead will look beneath for eternity, whilst the living memorise and hope for the unthinkable, life for me after death. I thought the bush of thorns would be where I would lie for all time but my frozen heart began to melt as a hand of human kindness lifted me from the thorns and terror. A hero gave me his heart unconditionally and took me into his family. It was as though I had been with them for a lifetime. You have to ask yourself is he the one I fell in love with and is it possible he is still by my side. Would fate take away my dream and heaven my child? Are we capable of deceiving you all? It makes sense to want to live our lives in peace and happiness. No matter what! Still the stories are told to hurt and deceive. Truth can be hidden for years. Over that time your imagination, like mine will work overtime.

Although I never age, my mind and imagination is always awake. Sometimes as the dark nights draw in, I can see myself going into a room. Inside this room is a large cauldron. The cauldron holds molten lead, beneath it is a fire burning to keep the lead in a liquid form. It is as though the room is a furnace as the walls glow like burning ember. I cannot breathe as the heat is attacking my whole body and the lead is beginning to affect my throat, I can even taste it! I turn quickly and go back through the door I came through. Only to find I was in a yard with rows and rows of white satin hanging on lines, flapping with fury as a strong breeze passed. The sun shone through the satin illuminating each sheet being whiter than white.

Beyond the lines of flapping satin were a group of tall figures, figures like humans. Like the white satin the sun shone through them. They had no faces and it's as though they were invisible. They surround a boat, like a wooden rowing boat with ornate oars, held by a figure in black, again with no face. Laying inside the boat was a coffin of lead with a crest on top. It is a crest I recognise. The tall invisible figures, seemed to be offering a coin to the figure in black. It reminded me of the stories of the ferryman who was always paid for taking man's soul to the other side, after they had passed over from this world, who knows maybe he was. He and the figures turned around as if to look at me and a flash of light appeared before me. It became a ball and in that ball was a cave. It had a red hue with rainbows of colour twinkling all over. There was a rock table in the middle. On the table was a time glass, measuring the sands of time. By the side was a book, it was my book of life as it had my name on with date of birth and another date. Which was the year you all thought I died. There was no cover on this book only parchment paper. Although I could read the title it was only written in numbers. That I find strange.

The walls of rainbow colours began to flicker, I looked closer and could see the colours held masks of many nations. I took one off the wall and put it on only to see many people of many nations sitting together in a cathedral. Then I heard music playing, it echoed with time. I even thought I could hear that music that haunts me. People were singing some crying. I even heard voices raised in anger. At that moment one of those tall invisible figures stood by me and took my hand. I looked at my hand and could only see the lines, they seemed to be deep rivers of emotion, "would they ever disappear?"

The figure never spoke it didn't have to. It's as though its thoughts passed through my mind of imagination. It was telling me there is a war of the heavens and throughout time heaven is recalling the earth angels for they are the weapons of love to counteract evil. I was part of heavens plan. Had my imagination turned me into an angel?

A huge flash appeared in the sky it was as though the sun had exploded. The light rays rushed towards the earth making all of mankind flee and hide into the depth of the earth. But no one would be safe from heavens wrath.

The tall figure seemed to take away all of my fear, then would you believe my whole life came before me as though it was a film replay.

With that and a blink of an eye I am back in my time warp! Waiting for autumn to drop her blanket of leaves to warm the earth, so it can move on and let the cold winter season take over nature.

Outside Looking In

Over the years many winter months have passed by and December is an exciting time for me as I always visit my home land at Christmas. It is a time I want to be near my family and children.

I long for the cold months to get colder as I want the snowflakes to fall from heaven and leave a soft white carpet covering the land with perfection. It is a happy memory of my lost childhood. Even to this day when I see it I want to dance with glee, jump and mess it all up. Childhood memories very rarely disappear.

I have to travel north to visit my children. Every year, I wait by the gates of their home (which is like a castle) in the hope they can see me and each time they pass me by. They have never noticed me and now my little ones are men. I walk through the snow and reach the front door. I knocked and knocked but cannot hear any sound no one comes I turn to go back down the drive way only to see I have left no footprints in the snow. It was as though I was a mirror and someone hit me! My emotions had shattered and broken into pieces.

Then within a second I was looking in a lead glass window. It was bow shaped and huge. Looking out from that window was a Christmas tree, it was filled with the prettiest decorations and lights like candles burning bright. On the top of the tree was a golden star. The Christmas spirit had filled the window. It is a tree that seems to be there every year and every year by my side, like me, outside looking in is a ghostly figure of a man, maybe a little older than myself. He takes my hand and the warmth is incredible. We pass no words to each other but he seems to tell me he was an RAF pilot in the second world war and he is my eldest sons guardian and his child will be his namesake. I wanted to know why he stood by me only to imagine, his earthly life was a mystery like mine. He then disappears only to leave one set of footprints in the snow by my side, I felt blessed to know this man. Who was he? I turn to look back in the window and there were my family and children taking presents and passing them around from the bottom of the Christmas tree. I wondered if they would find mine. There now! They have it, it is a snowflake from heaven filled with my love. From the multitude of falling snowflakes, my snowflake, my gift fell inside of the room between the Christmas tree and window. Everyone ran over to the window with joy to see the snow outside. My children touched my gift, it burst and melted, leaving joy and happiness. They shared this gift and came to look outside at the dark sky dropping her snowflakes. Or did they look for me? I turned to walk away with tears of angels rolling down my cheeks, knowing my children had touched my gift. I turned just to see their faces once more, they were looking down at the footprints outside the window as another set was by the side of my ghostly pilot. They were my footprints!

Walking away towards the gatehouse of my children's home, so many thoughts entered my mind. It was as though I needed more answers as I am confused as to my being. When I was looking through the window, why did no one notice me and ask me to join the festivities. Was my divorce a sentence, never to share a family Christmas with my children? Surely not! How could a sentence last so long? Now my children are men, they must have their own choice. The gift I left for them did they really touch it and did they see my footprints in the snow. Am I a ghost only to be seen by the pure of heart where am I, who am I, where has time gone to? How did I get here? Fear of not knowing made me begin to run. Running, running like the tiger that sees all. I race across the world. Never touching the land or splashing the sea. Maybe I was running through the sky, the music of the universe travelled with me through time. I watch the tears of angels fall into the earth's ocean creating tidal surges, threatening the earths land. I keep running not looking back or resting as I feel I am being hunted by man, like the tiger who sees all. The hunters have taken her cubs and like me my children. I become the lonely tiger of the night, searching for a resting place to evade the hunters. It comes into view, a circle of light from the sun's rays, making a halo of light around the golden shore. I stop running and my feet touch the sanctuary, it's my island. I can now rest, I am safe. My winter journey makes me wonder if heaven is my home. After all who but an angel would leave a gift of a snowflake? There are times, I feel as though I live in a world, within a world. I become closed in with my thoughts nothing seems to make sense, my ideas are far stretched as I see images which to me at this time becomes reality. I feel as though I have been locked in my room, in which I sleep.

I am frantic to get out. I begin to review my situation of past tragic events and what the real truth was. I start to shout wanting answers, hoping someone will hear to put my mind at rest.

How could an accident take so many lives? Who told me everyone except one died? How did I get on my island and who put me there? Then came the dreadful smell, a sickly mousy aroma. It was all around and even on my body. My hearing became intense, it was as though I was given a lasting memory of my two earthly senses I turn my head, to see my white satin pillow. Was it made from the white satin on the lines in the yard? Is my room in which I sleep really my coffin. The man in black, who I thought to be the ferryman, did the figures in white pay him for another reason? What was the ornate carving on the handle of the oar? Was the man in black from a higher order? Was the accident really sinister and meant for me or maybe it was staged for my love and I a victim of circumstances. Where is my love, where is he. I see him with me on my island. Is that my intense imagination or is it his ghost, he wanting to be by my side for eternity. Have we become one? It all goes round and round in my head as though I am being driven mad. There is a loud explosion that comes from behind me. This brings me to my senses. I realize, maybe that's what others want me to think, insanity is a high price for anyone to pay for love. I hear the door unlock, I open it and step outside of the room, or am I stepping out of my coffin and haunting you all with those stories that never will rest. Have you guessed who I am yet? Can you help me escape from my confusion? Maybe you need more clues.

Unlike most I am pure blood and a lady in my own rights. I was or still am a formidable force to be reckoned with, hence my now situation, I am a mother who even to this day will watch over my children, whether it be from heaven or earth. I am protective like the tiger of the night. Then there are the children who are not mine by birth but by need, I am their guardian and now my birth children are their carers. My young warriors have inherited my compassion and love. Only one of my warrior sons will be able to fulfill my dreams. How on earth do I know that?

There are so many incidents out there that make me believe I really am still here, on earth. Otherwise who would be writing this story? Pure imagination maybe!

Mother Nature

Once there was a man of a holy order, who took me into a room which looked like a room at the back of an old church. Its décor was just bricks with a coloured lead window, which looked over the countryside of my old home. He sits at a desk like a table, which holds a golden cross, with two candlesticks with white candles (alight) held by rose clasps. Also on the table is a parchment book. It looks like the book of my life, that was in the cavern.

He asks me to take a seat, I felt as though my father was sitting in the chair by my side. Holding a pen in his left hand, he begins to calculate the date of my birth and the date of my supposing death, dividing the total into the amount of my living days. This man of the holy order finishes the mathematical calculations and then begins to write the answer in an invisible book. He looks at me and shakes his head, telling me there is nothing he can do, as the numbers of my birth and death correspond with the date of the tragic event. It was the time for me of great changes.

I felt as though my father was horrified, but pleased I would be with him. Without any spoken words my father seemed to be questioning the man of the holy order, only to be told the major change on that day is beyond mans knowledge and only heaven can change the events and outcome. It was a sentence of death, I was mortified and afraid. I tried to hold my father's hand but he had vanished. I looked all around and even outside, where was he? I went back and asked the holy man could I be with my father, by his side. His refusal was sharp and he blew out the candles. His breath blew so strong it lifted me off the floor and into darkness. Once again I was on that island of nothing. It was just as damp and murky as before. I couldn't cry or move, I just wonder if the holy man was the breath of time!

The strangest thing is that I seemed to look down on the island of nothing, as though I was levitating, looking into the earth, only to see an empty coffin. That coffin with the crest on. I heard a rumble, like thunder and looked above only to see winters chariots of clouds racing across the sky, drawing in spring. One chariot stopped and hovered above me and from it stepped out Mother Nature. She was as royal as a queen, in fact she is and always will be the nature queen. Her gown was made of the tiniest snowdrops sewn together with gossamer thread. With dark hair that was the length of the snow white gown, which seemed to fall over the earth. Her earthly crown was a mixture of the spring flowers which was scattered all over her hair. The spring flowers and white snow was a design out of this world.

She took my hand and together we stepped into the chariot. A gust of wind so strong took us back above the earth to catch up with the other chariots. They were driven by the seeds of the earth who scattered themselves over lands and seas as they raced with the winds.

The nature queen only changed her emotions with the seasons but she was angry that heaven and earth left me alone on an island of nothing. In anger she began to race against the wind and rain, leaving them bewildered, not knowing which way the nature queen would turn. As she change her seasons. Her chariot clouds became an army of force on standby. She had declared war. Heaven surrendered, knowing that the angels had shed many tears for me and also they knew the might of the nature queen. I was given the right to be by my father's side.

Earth prepared for war as man was her ruler and he was stubborn not realizing earth was part of the nature queen's creation and she knew of earth's weakness.

The mightiest allies of the queen nature was the moon and the sea. She asked the moon to pull the sea tide and the sea to rise above the low level lands knowing man had not the knowledge to protect himself and the earth. No one ever realized the destruction it would cause, not one could stop the nature queen's fury.

The winds and the rain found a way to blow by the side of her chariot clouds. Together they swept over the world leaving a trail of destruction. The fire in the sky with a thundery noise joined in the rampage. People fled in terror and that was only a gentle touch of the nature queen's force. Thus man and earth relented and surrendered not wanting to see her in full fury.

The nature queen then knew I would be safe to be on the earth. The knowing whether I am alive or dead would be for my keeper and guardians to decide. I stepped out of her chariot and she was gone with the wind.

I am once again on my island of happiness. The force of the nature queen's anger seemed to have passed over my island leaving it untouched. Maybe my island of happiness is Shangri-la.

Now we have to find out who I am. It is not my decision but yours. What I write will make you become my guardian, if you choose! What you read makes you become my keeper. As you have the ability to unlock the door to many hidden secrets. You hold the key of life, my life, if you cannot find it look towards the great pyramids where the sands of time rise like great mountains. These mountainous dunes will fall to reveal a great city, unlike any seen on this earth.

The city has been molded and built out of an unknown metal. Beneath the circular shapes are the stones of the universe. They depict the planets that holds life and some would say they hold mans soul.

There is a silver river running through the city that holds no life and never did. It was a river to protect the city. By the side of the river is a tower, inside hanging down, a bell rope holds a key. Take the key and open the door, with an inscription (Gift of Kings), there you will find a long box with four drawers. Look into each drawer. Maybe in one you will find your answer.

When you open your first drawer the contents will take your breath away. It is filled with jewels fit for a queen. The gem stones are the most precious. There are diamonds, rubies, emeralds and sapphires, ready, waiting to be set in an unfinished crown. A crown that was to be for a lost queen.

The ruby from the east, of enormous size was her blood. The emeralds her tears of loneliness, the sapphires the colour of her eyes and the diamonds were the stones that wounded her heart. I could well be that lost queen! What do you think? Lost on earth, maybe!

Open the second drawer there are documents of births, deaths and marriages. Letters of love all jumbled up with dreams of yesterday. If you try to read what is written, you will find the writing will disappear. Only your imagination would be able to see. "Oh look!" There is a photograph of me, with my name written on, as if it is an autograph, see! see! Sorry it has gone. It was just my imagination.

The third drawer was empty as it held the ghosts of the earth, which no one can see. Except maybe the pure of heart. Put your hand in and it will tell you if I have passed you and the world by. It would also mean I am a ghost haunting life. Oh! Maybe you should keep your hands out.

The last drawer is the fourth, it holds books. Books of fact based fantasy and mystery. Look through them if you choose one to read, you are my keeper and have that ability to open up a book and reveal who I am and the truth about my life. Read it and you will become my guardian and have the knowing to place me where you wish me to be.

So tell me who is the Mother of Kings? Who am I? Where am I? A book of mystery or fantasy, my imagination or yours? A ghost of the earth, wandering waiting to be put to rest. Or a lost queen. You know! Tell me! Tell me!

Lightning Source UK Ltd.
Milton Keynes UK
UKOW06f0003010715

254344UK00011B/209/P